Friddy Forever

by

Annie Dalton

Illustrated by Brett Hudson

You do not need to read this page - just get on with the book!

Published in 2002 in Great Britain by
Barrington Stoke Ltd
10 Belford Terrace, Edinburgh EH4 3DQ

This edition based on *Friday Forever*, published by Barrington Stoke in 2001

ISBN 1-84299-070-5

Printed by Polestar AUP Aberdeen Ltd

MEET THE AUTHOR - ANNIE DALTON

What is your favourite animal?
Deer
What is your favourite boy's name?
Reuben
What is your favourite girl's name?
Anna and Maria, my daughters
What is your favourite food?
Lemon pudding
What is your favourite music?
All kinds!
What is your favourite hobby?
Watching films

MEET THE ILLUSTRATOR - BRETT HUDSON

What is your favourite animal?
Wombat
What is your favourite boy's name?
Josh
What is your favourite girl's name?
Lindsey
What is your favourite food?
Thai curry
What is your favourite music?
Anything
What is your favourite hobby?
Travelling

To Maria
A big thank you for coming up with
the idea for *Friday Forever*

Contents

1   The Cosmic Burp   1

2   Lenny Stresses Out   5

3   Too Much Pressure   11

4   Friday 4 Ever   23

5   Trapped in Time   37

6   Miss Parrot's Book Quiz   45

7   It's Never Too Late!   59

8   Lenny Changes History   71

Chapter 1
The Cosmic Burp

It all began with a rush of wind, a burp, a huge, cosmic burp ...

What a mad way to begin a story!

"YUCK!" you say. What kind of joker starts his story with a *cosmic* burp?

And all you kids who like science are saying, a COSMIC burp? There's NO such thing! A nasty tummy upset, that's all it was.

But I want you all to hang on in there. Without the burp, my story won't make sense. Trust me.

Did you know that everything happens for a reason? It's true of everything in the universe, from black holes to cosmic burps.

Everything has to come from somewhere.

So where do cosmic burps come from? In a word?

STRESS!

Lenny Brown was a boy under major stress.

And who's Lenny Brown?

Don't you know *anything*?

It's me, you dummy! This is my story.

This is the story of the day which changed my life.

Chapter 2
Lenny Stresses Out

Have you ever seen someone blow up a balloon, then let it go? It zooms around the room like crazy.

Well, that's how I felt inside. I felt as if I had a balloon inside me. A balloon that was WAY too full of air.

If I wasn't careful, the balloon might go zooming out of control. I might do something REALLY mad.

I was under stress. MAJOR stress. And where did that stress come from? Do you have to ask? My parents, of course!

Mum and Dad got at me all the time. "Get your act together, Lenny! Shape up, Lenny! LENNY! Get a grip, Lenny!"

This was what they said to me every day before school.

Then I'd walk into our classroom and our teacher, Mr Carter, would start. "Wipe that grin off your face, boy! Do you think life is one big *joke*?"

And all the time, my stress balloon was getting bigger and bigger. Why couldn't people leave me alone? I wasn't bad. I didn't nick things from shops. I liked to have a bit of fun, that's all.

My parents had no right to tell me what to do. My mum and dad couldn't even AGREE about anything. Dad wanted me to be a famous footballer. That's what *he* wanted to

be at my age. I do love sports, but I'm not that good. But Dad said I didn't try. He said I was lazy. He said I'd never get anywhere in life.

Mum wanted me to be famous too. A famous artist. But I can't draw to save my life!

I knew that Mum and Dad felt I was letting them down. So did my teacher, Mr Carter.

Why else did they nag me all the time? "You just don't try, Lenny. Wake *up*, Lenny!" they kept telling me.

Wake up? I was about to EXPLODE!

And that's what I did.

Chapter 3
Too Much Pressure

The date was FRIDAY, 23 MAY.

I opened my eyes. A funky little tune was playing on the radio in the kitchen. I can remember every little thing from that morning. The sound of rain on my window. The smell of burnt toast.

I looked at the clock. Yessss! Friday at last! Just one more day, then I'd have a whole weekend to do what I liked!

I dashed down to the kitchen. There was a blue haze in the air. "Mu-um! You burnt the toast," I said.

Mum dumped some black toast in the bin. "You'll have to eat cornflakes," she said.

She looked different. Not like my mum at all. She had posh clothes on. She was even wearing make-up.

"I hate cornflakes," I said.

When I tipped up the packet, five cornflakes fell out. I gave up on breakfast and went to find my football strip. I found it in the wash-basket with the mud still on it!

I had good days and bad days, high stress days and low stress days. This was going to be a high stress day.

I felt the balloon swell inside me. I lost my temper. "You know I need my games kit on Friday," I yelled at Mum.

"Sorry, love," said Mum. "I did mean to wash it. But I was so nervous about this job, I forgot."

"What are you on about?" I said. "You haven't got a job!"

Do I look silly?

"Not yet. But I'm hoping to get one today."

"Oh," I said. "That's why you've got those silly clothes on. You look like a TV presenter."

I was sorry as soon as I said it. I didn't mean to upset Mum. It was the stress talking, not me.

Suddenly, I saw my mates Dave and Andy making mad faces through the window.

I grabbed my muddy football strip and rushed out.

On the way to school, Dave told a joke about a dead rabbit. Andy laughed so much, he kicked his football into someone's garden.

A cross, old man came out and yelled at us for messing up his gravel.

Andy and Dave ran off laughing.

But the old man caught me by my hood. He wouldn't let me go until I'd raked his gravel for him. And it was raining!

I zipped my jacket up under my chin. I was wet, and that cross old man had made me late for school.

By the time I got to school, the playground was empty.

Someone came up behind me. It was
Ross, a boy from my class. He's so sad.

We dashed to our classroom. I didn't
talk to Ross and he didn't talk to me. Cool
kids like me and nerds like Ross don't mix
at our school. And Ross wasn't just a nerd.
He was a disaster on two legs.

17

On rainy days the floors get slippery.
Ross skidded on the wet floor and fell flat
on his face. I had to laugh. I couldn't help it.

Our teacher, Mr Carter, was off sick.
That day we had a student teacher. She
wore a pink, fluffy cardigan and had long,
blonde hair.

"My name is Miss Parrot," she told the class. "And we have a new boy today called Darren."

"I ADORE student teachers," said Dave.

"Yeah," I agreed. "You can skive all day long."

Sita heard us. "You boys are sick," she said.

A wasp flew in through the window. One of the girls gave a yell.

"I hate wasps, Miss!"

Darren, the new boy, was scared. "I'm allergic to wasps. I swell up if I get stung, Miss."

"Oh, dear!" said Miss Parrot. She flapped at the wasp.

Dave and I grinned at each other. "We'll help, Miss," said Dave.

"Yeah, Miss," I said. "You're safe with us."

And so we helped Miss Parrot. We sent chairs and books flying. We jumped on desks.

The wasp zoomed over to the new boy, just as if it KNEW he was allergic to wasp stings.

Sita sighed. "I'll get it, Miss." And she caught the wasp in a paper cup and put it out of the window.

Chapter 4
Friday 4 Ever

My mates thought that Sita was a teacher's pet, because she got top marks. I thought she was quite cool, for a girl.

At break I heard her singing with her mates. It was the funky tune I'd heard on the radio that morning.

Darren was too new to have any mates. He watched us play football. Once he kicked the ball back to us. It was a really cool kick.

I was going to ask Darren if he wanted to play. But Dave said, "That new kid is such a wimp. He was scared of a WASP."

So I didn't say anything.

At lunch, Ross had another disaster. Andy bumped into him and Ross dropped his tray of food. He had to pick his chips up off the floor. He was almost crying.

"Look at the little piggy eating off the floor," said Dave.

"Want some ketchup with that, piggy?" Andy said. And he tipped ketchup all over Ross's dirty chips.

I should have felt sorry for Ross, but I had problems of my own. Something was going on inside my chest. I couldn't breathe. My balloon was getting bigger and bigger. I had to let some of the stress out or I'd burst.

I took the ketchup from Andy. But I didn't tip it over Ross's chips. I tipped it over Ross.

The stress inside me died down, just like that. I began to laugh. *It's gone*! I thought. *It's gone and it won't come back*!

The dinner ladies didn't see us teasing Ross. But Sita did. She sees everything. She gave Ross a tissue to wipe his face and put half her chips on his plate. Then she walked

Those bullies won't get away with it!

right past me. She didn't talk to me or even look at me.

I pretended I didn't care about Sita. "We're the kings of this school!" I said to my mates.

After lunch, we had football. Darren didn't try out for the team in the end. No-one had told him to bring his kit. He just had to sit and watch. He looked upset.

But I forgot about Darren. I was on brilliant form. In the last half I scored the winning goal!

My mates carried me to the changing rooms. I felt like a hero.

I wish the day had ended then and there.

It was bad luck that we had Art with Miss Parrot after that. I don't think she'd taught kids our age before. She'd put out paper and foil and gold stars and pink hearts, as if we were toddlers.

"We're going to make collages," she said. "Does everyone know what a collage is?"

We shook our heads. But Sita knew. "You glue things onto paper to make pictures," she said.

What!! I thought. No *way*!

Bam! My stress was back. But it didn't feel like a balloon that was going to burst. It felt like a time-bomb going tick, tick, tick, tick. A bomb that was getting ready to go off.

That's why I played a mean trick on Miss Parrot.

I had to. The stress made me do it.

When Miss Parrot found her books all covered in glue, she went bananas. "Who did this?" she yelled.

I looked at my mates and my mates looked at me.

Then we all pointed to Ross.

"It's him, Miss. He glued your books," I said. "Look at his hands. They're all sticky."

Ross stared at Miss Parrot in horror. "I didn't glue your books, Miss!"

Miss Parrot thought he was lying. She sent Ross off to see the headmaster.

"You've made a big mistake!" Sita told her. "Ross wouldn't do something like that."

"I'm the teacher, thank you, Sita," said Miss Parrot in a cold voice. "One more word from you and you'll stay in after school."

I'd got away with it!

You'd think I'd feel happy. But I didn't. The bomb in my chest was ticking faster now.

Ten, nine, eight ...

It was going to explode. Relax, Lenny! I told myself. You're just having fun. You're king of the school. You're a star!

My mates were giving me funny looks.

Seven, six, five ...

"Are you feeling OK?" said Andy. "Because you look weird."

Four, three, two ...

"Me? I'm fine!" I said. "I've had a brilliant day! I wish my life was always this cool. I wish it could be Friday for ever!"

WHOOOOOSH!!

All my stress came rushing out in one huge, cosmic burp. Scraps of paper and tin foil flew up into the air. Gold stars and pink hearts flew around me.

Everyone was looking at me.

Dave's mouth fell open. "What was *that*?"

Sita looked at me with disgust. "That wasn't clever and it wasn't funny," she said.

I didn't care. All my stress had gone. I felt BRILLIANT.

Then all my scraps of paper and foil and stars and hearts came down again. And they formed a message on the table beside me.

I rubbed my eyes. When I looked again, the message had gone.

When I got home, our house smelled like an old bonfire. Mum had burned the chicken pie. I was SO fed up. "What am I going to eat, then?" I yelled at her.

"I don't know, do I?" Mum yelled back and she rushed to her room.

I had to watch TV by myself till Dad came home.

Dad went upstairs to talk to Mum. "She's not feeling well," he said when he came down. "I think she's upset she didn't get that job."

I'd forgotten all about Mum's job. "She doesn't have to take it out on us," I said.

Dad made us beans on toast. But it wasn't the same as Mum's chicken pie.

After tea, I went to my room to play with my computer, but I couldn't keep my mind on it. The house didn't feel like home. It was full of bad smells and bad vibes.

I felt worn out, so I thought I'd go to bed early.

I got into bed, and turned off my alarm clock. I didn't want to miss my Saturday lie-in!

I closed my eyes. Bliss!

****

DING-A-LING-A-LING!

My stupid alarm clock went off as usual. "Shut up!" I said. "It's Saturday!"

I threw my clock across the room. How could my alarm get me up on a Saturday?

I could hear rain on my window.
A funky little tune was playing on the radio in the kitchen.

There was a smell of burnt toast.

I felt scared. Something didn't add up.

What's going on? I thought. Mum never gets up this early on Saturday. I looked at my clock. I picked it up and shook it. Then I shook it again.

But it still said Friday. FRIDAY, 23 MAY.

**FRIDAY
23 MAY
7:30**

Chapter 5
Trapped in Time

I put on my clothes and looked at myself in the mirror. I looked the same, but I didn't feel the same. I felt as if I was an actor playing at being me. I felt odd and shaky.

I went downstairs. The kitchen was full of blue smoke. There was Mum in her posh clothes, dumping burnt toast in the bin.

Was this Mum's idea of a joke? If so, it wasn't very funny.

"What's going on?" I said. I was really scared now.

"You'll have to have cornflakes," Mum began.

"I'm not talking about the toast," I yelled. "What day is it today?"

"Friday, of course. Why?"

The hairs stood up on my arms. This was creepy. "So – so if it's Friday why didn't you wash my football kit?" I yelled. "It's still here, look!" I was shaking all over.

"Sorry, love," said Mum. "I did mean to wash them, but I was nervous about this job and I forgot – "

"Stop it!" I yelled. "Is this an action replay or something?"

"What do you mean?" said Mum.

She had no idea what I was on about. Suddenly, I saw my mates Dave and Andy making mad faces outside the window. Was this a sick joke?

It's a bad dream, I thought. I've got to wake up. I pinched my arm. "Ouch!!!" It hurt. This wasn't a dream. It was real.

My mates were waiting. I had to walk to school with them as if it was a normal day.

On the way to school, Dave told that joke about a dead rabbit. I felt sick with fear. The same things were happening all over again in the same order. The same cross old man grabbed my hood, we had the same new student teacher, the same wasp.

It was like an action replay of yesterday. And there was nothing I could do. Everyone else seemed to think it was just another school day.

But it wasn't. It was yesterday. *Again*.

After lunch I put glue on Miss Parrot's books. Ross got the blame and Sita stood up for him. All over again.

When I got home the house smelled of burning. My heart sank. I'd forgotten about the chicken pie.

I yelled at Mum and she rushed up to her room. I went to bed in a house full of bad smells and bad vibes.

I turned off the lamp. "Whew, that was weird," I said. "I've never heard of a person's day happening all over again!"

My second Friday was over, that was the important thing. Tomorrow was Saturday. I could sleep in!

A few hours later my alarm went off.

A funky tune was playing on the radio in the kitchen. It was raining and the smell of burnt toast came up from below.

I looked at the clock, but I knew what I'd see.

I got out of bed like a zombie. I began to get dressed. Then my knees gave way and I had to sit down again.

It was Friday all over again. I was trapped in a time-loop and I couldn't get out!

Chapter 6
Miss Parrot's Book Quiz

For the first few Fridays, I got through the school day like someone in a dream.

"I've got to get out of this," I'd tell myself. And I'd try to work out what had happened.

I'd made a stupid wish. One I didn't really mean. And a weird cosmic burp had sent my wish zooming off into space.

One silly wish =
DiSASTER

Had someone out there heard my wish? But wishes don't really come true. Or do they?

I was sure of one thing. My burp had somehow pressed a REPLAY button and I was trapped in time. I'd never have another holiday, never have Christmas or birthday presents. Never grow up and leave home.

There would be no more surprises, ever. I would have to lie in the dark, in a house filled with bad smells and bad vibes.

Friday forever. FRIDAY FOREVER.

It was like an evil spell.

I was twelve years old and my life was over.

****

One Friday I was again raking the old man's gravel, AGAIN.

Suddenly, I started to smile. Cheer up, Lenny, I told myself. Being down is not your style.

There and then I decided to make a few changes.

Next day, when Andy and Dave came to my house, they stared at me in surprise.

"Where did you get that hat, Lenny?" said Andy.

"It's my new look," I said.

On the way to school, Dave began to tell the dead rabbit joke.

"Don't tell that joke, whatever you do," I said, in a spooky voice.

Dave looked blank. "Why?"

"Because I know what's going to happen next."

"No, you don't," said Andy.

"Yes, I do. Your stupid joke is going to make me late for school."

Dave just looked at me.

"OK, *don't* believe me," I said. "And by the way, Mr Carter's off sick today. We've got a student teacher called Miss Parrot. And there's a new kid. His name's Darren and he's allergic to wasps."

My mates thought I was joking. I wish you'd seen their faces when it all happened just like I said.

News of my magic powers went round the school in no time. Girls were coming up to me, begging me to tell their fortunes.

Later, at lunch, Sita gave me a funny look. "What's your game?" she said. "I know you, Lenny Brown. You're up to something."

At that moment, Ross dropped his chips on the floor and Andy began tipping ketchup on them.

But I was suddenly sick of action replays. I walked out of the hall. I kept on walking all the way back home.

I knew I wouldn't get suspended for bunking off. Tomorrow would be Friday again, just like today. No-one would remember a thing!

Then it hit me. I'd got what I'd always wanted.

I was free! For the first time in my life there was no stress. I could do what I liked.

And no-one could stop me!

****

The next few Fridays were great! I did all the things I'd always wanted to do. I ran up and down the stairs and set off all the fire alarms. I let the hamsters out of their cages.

I was so out of order that Dave and Andy couldn't keep up with me.

TWO WAYS TO TEASE A TEACHER

Set off the fire alarm!

Let the hamsters out!

It's not much fun being bad on your own. You get tired. And you start to running out of ideas.

****

One morning, I woke up and I just couldn't drag myself out of bed.

"You must be getting the flu," said Mum. "I think you should stay home today."

After she'd gone off, I came down and watched a video until she came back. Then I went back to bed again.

This went on for *days.*

Then one morning I saw myself in the mirror. I looked sick and pale.

Next day, Dave and Andy came to get me. "I've really missed you guys!" I said. But they didn't know I'd been off school!

That day, it was the same old story. Sita got rid of the wasp. Miss Parrot gave us an English lesson.

Oh, didn't I tell you we had an English lesson? That's because I didn't listen in class. But today, for the first time, I did.

Miss Parrot gave us a quiz on a book that Mr Carter had read with us.

Ross and Sita got nine out of ten. Darren, the new boy, got seven. He'd read the book at his old school. I got two out of ten. Well, I'd never even *looked* at the book. For the first time, I felt bad about this.

That night, after tea, I read the book. It was OK once you got into it.

Next day, I *did* try to do the quiz. And do you know, I only got five out of ten!

I was SO fed up. That night, I read that book again and took notes.

It took me two more Fridays and then ...

"Well done, Lenny!" smiled Miss Parrot. "You got top marks."

I acted like I didn't care, but I was on a high. Wow, I thought. Top marks! That's so cool!

I tried to remember the last time a teacher had said something good about me. All I could come up with was one time when I got a gold star in Year 1.

I was shocked. It couldn't be *that* long ago. Could it?

Chapter 7
It's Never Too Late!

I'd got the book quiz sorted, so I thought I'd start on history. We were doing the Second World War.

It wasn't hard. Miss Parrot told us the same facts and dates every day. I got out some books from the library, in case I needed back-up info.

Soon I was calling out the answers to Miss Parrot's questions before Sita could open her mouth. Life was looking up!

Now I had a new problem. My diet. Every day it was burgers and beans, burgers and beans. That CAN'T be good for you.

One night, I had a dream that I was eating *salad*. I was gutted when I woke up and found it wasn't true!

At lunchtime the next day, I felt ill just looking at my burger. "I need some air," I told my mates.

On the way out, I saw Darren. He was eating lunch all by himself. He looked lonely.

When you have to live the same day over and over again, you see things you missed the first time round.

This time, I didn't walk past Darren.
I stopped and spoke to him. "I've seen you
play football," I said. "You're OK."

"Oh, thanks," he said.

"They're trying out for the school team today," I went on. "It's your first day, so I bet you didn't know to bring your kit."

Darren looked upset. "No-one told me."

"Don't panic. Is anyone at home?"

"My mum," he said.

"Ask them in the school office if you can use the phone. Tell your mum you need your kit and she can drop it off for you."

Darren smiled. "I'll do that. Thanks, Lenny." He raced off to the office.

That afternoon, Darren was rushing up and down the football pitch with a big grin on his face.

In the last half, I scored the winning goal, like always. But then, do you know what?

Darren scored a second goal!

"Yessss!" I punched the air. Then I rushed over and rubbed Darren's head. I was over the moon.

Want to know why? For the first time in weeks of Fridays, something had *changed*!

****

After school, I told Dave and Andy to go home without me. I needed to be by myself. I said I had to go shopping for Mum. I needed time to think.

I hadn't gone far when I saw Ross on the other side of the road with his little sister. I was surprised. Ross looked relaxed and happy. Then he saw me, tripped and fell in the gutter. He got up looking really miserable.

That's what happens when you live the same day over and over again. You see little things you didn't see before.

Ross wasn't a disaster on two legs. He was scared. He was scared of Andy and Dave. And me.

Ross thought I was a bully. When I was around, he just lost it.

I felt gutted. I'd been telling myself it was stress that made me mean.

Now I saw that this was an excuse. I saw that other people were under stress just like me.

When I got home, I was greeted by the smell of burning. Mum was in the kitchen throwing the chicken pie into the bin. She looked tired and unhappy. Mum was stressed too.

"You look as if you could do with a cup of tea," I said. Making tea isn't my thing, but I plugged in the kettle and found the milk and teabags as if I did it every day.

"So did you get the job?" I asked.

"Don't ask! I was crazy to think I could go back to work. I've left it too late."

"Rubbish," I said. "It's never too late." I handed her a mug of tea.

I found myself telling her about my day. I missed out the fact that for me it was always Friday these days. It was the best chat I'd had with my mum for ages.

She drank the tea. "Thanks, Lenny," she said. "You've really cheered me up." She tried to smile. "Tell you what, let's order a pizza. We'll have a nice night in and watch silly videos."

"Great. This is what I want for my topping," I told Mum. "Extra cheese, ham, sweetcorn ..."

"Slow down!" laughed Mum. "You'd think I'd been starving you."

"And, er, Mum," I said, "could you ask them to send a salad with that? A very large green salad?"

That night I couldn't sleep. No, I hadn't eaten too much pizza. My mind was working over-time. When I first got trapped in time, I could only think of three ways to deal with my problem.

1.   I could switch off and just drift through the endless Fridays, as if it was all a dream.

2.   I could trash the joint. Be a bad boy.

3.   I could run away from it all. Stay home. Play sick.

But now I'd found another way out.

I could *change* things!

If you got it right, changing things was like a magic power. Just by missing out on lunch, I'd changed a lot.

I'd helped Darren and look what happened! Our team scored not one goal, but two.

Then, when I got home, I was nice to my mum. I gave her tea and cheered her up.

Tonight, our house felt like a home again. The bad vibes had gone.

Tonight, I went to bed full of pizza and salad.

Tonight, Mum and Dad were down there laughing at some silly video.

Just one, tiny change had led to all these other changes.

But that wasn't why I was lying wide awake.

I'd had a fantastic idea.

If changing one, small thing made such a huge difference, *what would happen if I changed everything?*

What then?

Chapter 8
Lenny Changes History

I made myself stay awake all night.
I kept the light on. I knew that if I went to
sleep, I wouldn't wake up until the alarm
went off. Then it would be too late to carry
out my plan.

Ten minutes before the alarm went off, I
got up, got dressed and went to the kitchen.

When Mum came in I was laying the table. "Flowers! A cloth on the table!" she said. "But it's not my birthday!"

"No, but you're going for this job today and I thought you could do with a boost."

I saw smoke coming out of the toaster and hit the button hard. Two slices of golden brown toast popped out. For the first time in weeks I was going to get some breakfast! "I'll butter yours," I told Mum.

"Lenny," Mum said when breakfast was over, "have you done something bad?"

"Look, I'd love to stay and chat," I said, "but I've got stuff to do. Tell my mates I'll see them at school, OK?" Then I added, "By the way, you look great today. Good luck with the job. I bet you'll knock them dead."

I did have stuff to do. I also thought I'd give Dave's rabbit joke a miss.

On the way to school, I saw the old man at his window. "Gravel's looking good!" I yelled.

He smiled at me. I ran off to wait for Ross. I hung about for ages before he showed up. I got soaking wet! At last I saw him coming down the street. When he saw me, he gave a big gulp.

"Hi," I said. "Like to walk to school with me?"

Ross didn't look very happy but he couldn't say no.

"Cheer up," I grinned, "this could be your lucky day."

"Yeah, I could get run over," said Ross. "Then I wouldn't have to go to school."

"I'm not joking," I told him. "Today could be fun."

"You're mad," said Ross. "How can school be fun?"

"I'll show you," I said.

We got to school on time. We didn't have to rush and Ross didn't fall over.

It's hard work changing things. But I stuck with it. I hung on in there all morning.

I didn't make the wasp angry. I helped Sita to catch it in the cup because I knew Darren was allergic.

I didn't want to make even more stress for everyone.

But how could I change that awful moment when Dave made Ross drop his lunch tray? How could I stop Andy from picking up the ketchup?

Lunchtime came. *You need a plan, Lenny,* I told myself. *You must have a plan.*

Then Dave knocked into Ross and he let go of his tray. It was raining chips everywhere.

And do you know what? I didn't have to think. Just as Andy was about to pick up the ketchup bottle, my hand shot out.

"No, you don't," I said in a firm voice.

Andy's mouth fell open. So did Dave's.

I smiled. "Ross doesn't like ketchup. Do you, Ross?"

Ross was smiling too. "No," he said. "But thanks for the offer." He went off as cool as anything.

Andy made a face. "Don't tell me you're planning to be best buddies with that nerd."

"Yes, I am," I said. "Ross is cool when you get to know him."

Sita passed us with her tray. I thought she was smiling.

Yikes! I thought, *I've forgotten about Darren*. I rushed off to remind him to ask his mum to bring his kit. It's hard work changing things. Could I do it?

The hardest part was still to come.

Every morning I had told myself that I would not glue the pages of poor Miss Parrot's books together. But every afternoon, some strange force drew me to that glue pot, and every day I played my stupid trick all over again.

Miss Parrot had set out all the collage stuff as she did every Friday. My heart sank. *Here we go*, I thought.

I didn't know what to do. So I just stayed where I was, and after a bit, I found myself sticking scraps of paper on the page.

Oh, what the hell, I thought. You did the book quiz. You got to be the class expert on the Second World War. Why not do the stupid collage?

After all, I'd said I was going to change everything. So I got started. And do you know what? I really got into it. I forgot where I was.

After a bit, someone was standing behind me. It was Sita. She gazed at my artwork and gave a big smile.

"This is so cool," she told everyone. "Lenny's put us all in his picture. That's me with the wasp! And there's Ross and Darren. And this is you, Miss, in your pink cardigan."

Miss Parrot came over to look at the collage.

"It's all the things that happened today," I told her.

She looked amazed. "But you've remembered every little thing."

I hid a secret smile. "Yes, Miss," I said. Then I knew what to do with my collage. "Take it, Miss," I said. "It's a present."

"You must put your name on it," said Sita. "Great artists always put their name on their work."

I wrote my name in fancy writing.

Then I looked up and saw the time. "It's half past three!" I yelled.

"Oh dear!" said Miss Parrot. "I've got a bus to catch."

I rushed over to Miss Parrot's desk. "Your books," I said. "Are you sure they're OK? No glue on them?"

"My books are fine!" laughed Miss Parrot. She threw them into her bag. Then she rushed off to catch her bus, taking my collage with her.

I walked home feeling really happy. But when I went home I got a big surprise. There were no bad cooking smells. There were no cooking smells at all.

"Hi," I said to Mum, "how's the chicken pie?"

"Oh, I didn't make one," she said.

"Oh, right," I said, with a gulp.

Mum was acting really cool. I wondered why.

"Aren't you going to ask me about my interview?" she said in the same, cool voice.

"Sure. Was it OK?" I asked.

She jumped up and threw her arms around me. "Yes! I got the job!"

"Wow, that's great!" I said. "So, er – can we phone for a pizza?" I wasn't being rude. I was just REALLY hungry.

"With the money I'll get?" said Mum. "No way."

"Oh, yeah, sorry," I said. "I wasn't thinking. So do you want me to cook some sausages or what?"

"No way!" Mum yelled. "I've booked us a table at the best place in town. I'm taking us all out to dinner! And it's OK," she added with a grin, "they do big salads, I checked."

I went to bed stuffed. I was worn out. I'd been awake for 24 hours.

I switched my alarm off, just out of habit, and fell fast asleep.

When I woke up, the sun was shining into my room. Kids played and yelled in the street. I could smell fresh coffee and toast.

Hang about, I thought. What's this?

Even then I didn't dare to hope.

I sat up and looked at my clock. When I saw what it said, I didn't know if I should laugh or cry.

It was 10.30 am on SATURDAY, 24 MAY.

My never-ending Friday was over at last!

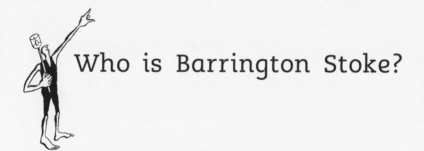

Who is Barrington Stoke?

Barrington Stoke went from place to place with his lamp in his hand. Everywhere he went, he told stories to children. Some were happy, some were sad, some were funny and some were scary.

The children always wanted more. When it got dark, they had to go home to bed. They went to look for Barrington Stoke the next day, but he had gone.

The children never forgot the stories. They told them to each other and to their children and their grandchildren. You see, good stories are magic and they can live forever.

If you loved this story, why don't you read ...

Wartman

by Michael Morpurgo

Have you ever had a wart? Dilly has one called George who causes him a lot of grief. Until that is, he meets old Mr Ben.

4u2read.ok!

You can order this book directly from Macmillan Distribution Ltd, Brunel Road, Houndmills, Basingstoke, Hampshire RG21 6XS   Tel: 01256 302699